This book belongs to

LIAM   HUTSON

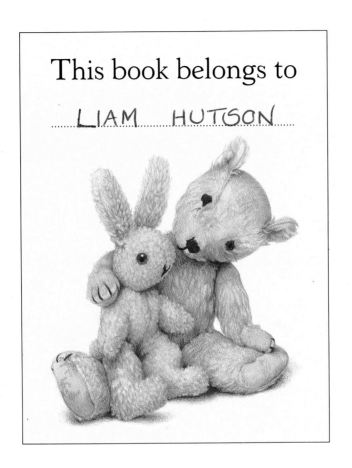

JANE HISSEY'S
OLD BEAR
STORIES

Old Bear

Little Bear's Trousers

Little Bear Lost

Jolly Tall

Jolly Snow

BCA

LONDON   NEW YORK   SYDNEY   TORONTO

This edition published 1994 by BCA
by arrangement with
Hutchinson Children's Books

CN 4000

Random House Australia (Pty) Limited
20 Alfred Street, Milsons Point, Sydney
New South Wales 2061, Australia

Random House New Zealand Limited
18 Poland Road, Glenfield
Auckland 10, New Zealand

Random House South Africa (Pty) Limited
PO Box 337, Bergvlei, South Africa

Random House UK Limited Reg. No. 954009

Printed in China

Old Bear

JANE HISSEY

IT wasn't anybody's birthday, but Bramwell Brown had a feeling that today was going to be a special day. He was sitting thoughtfully on the windowsill with his friends Duck, Rabbit and Little Bear when he suddenly remembered that someone wasn't there who should be.

A VERY long time ago, he had seen his good friend
Old Bear being packed away in a box. Then he
was taken up a ladder, through a trap door and into
the attic. The children were being too rough with
him and he needed somewhere safe to go for a while.

Hᴀꜱ he been forgotten, do you think?' Bramwell asked his friends.

'I think he might have been,' said Rabbit.

'Well,' said Little Bear, 'isn't it time he came back down with us? The children are older now and would look after him properly. Let's go and get him!'

'What a marvellous idea!' said Bramwell. 'But how can we rescue him? It's a long way up to the attic and we haven't got a ladder.'

'We could build a tower of bricks,' suggested Little Bear.

Rabbit collected all the bricks and the others set about building the tower. It grew very tall, and Little Bear was just putting on the last brick when the tower began to wobble.

'Look out!' he cried as the whole thing came tumbling down.

'Never mind,' said Bramwell, helping Little Bear to his feet. 'We'll just have to think of something else.'

L ET'S try making *ourselves* into a tower,' said Duck. 'Good idea!' said Bramwell.

Little Bear climbed on top of Rabbit's head and Rabbit hopped onto Duck's beak. They stretched up as far as they could, but then Duck opened his beak to say something, Rabbit wobbled, and they all collapsed on top of Bramwell.

'Sorry,' said Duck, 'perhaps that wasn't a very good idea.'

'Not one of your best,' replied Bramwell from somewhere underneath the heap.

I KNOW!' said Rabbit. 'Let's try bouncing on the bed.'

'Trust you to think of that,' said Bramwell. 'You never can resist a bit of bouncing, especially when it's not allowed.'

Rabbit climbed on to the bed and began to bounce up and down. The others joined him. They bounced higher and higher but *still* they couldn't reach the trap door in the ceiling.

Duck began to cry. 'Oh dear,' he sobbed. 'What are we going to do now? We'll never be able to rescue Old Bear and he'll be stuck up there getting lonelier and lonelier for ever and ever.'

'We mustn't give up,' said Bramwell firmly. 'Come on, Little Bear, you're good at ideas.'

But Little Bear had already noticed the plant in the corner of the room.

I'VE got it!' he cried. 'I could climb up this plant, swing from the leaves, kick the trap door open and jump in!'

In case it wobbled, Bramwell Brown, Duck and Rabbit steadied the pot. Little Bear bravely climbed up the plant until he reached the very top leaf. He took hold of it and started to swing to and fro, but he swung so hard that the leaf broke and he went crashing down. Luckily, Bramwell Brown was right underneath to catch him in his paws.

'That was a rotten idea,' said Little Bear.

'What I was thinking,' said Duck, 'was that it is a pity I can't fly very well, as I could have been quite a help.'

'Ah ha!' said Bramwell. 'That, my dear Duck, has given me a very good idea. I really think this one might work.'

IN the corner of the playroom was a little wooden aeroplane with a propeller that went round and round.

'We could use this plane to get to the trap door,' said Bramwell. 'Rather dangerous, I know, but quite honestly I can't bear to think of Old Bear up there alone for a minute longer.'

'I'll be pilot,' said Rabbit, hopping up and down, making aeroplane noises.

'And I'll stand on the back and push the trap door open with my paintbrush,' said Little Bear.

'But how will you get down?' asked Duck.

'I've already thought of that,' said Bramwell, who hadn't really but quickly did. 'They can use these handkerchiefs as parachutes and we'll catch them in a blanket.'

BRAMWELL gave Little Bear two big handkerchiefs and a torch so he could see into the attic. Then he began to wind up the propeller of the plane. Rabbit and Little Bear climbed aboard and Bramwell began the countdown: 'Five! Four! Three! Two! One! ZERO!'

They were off! The plane whizzed along the carpet and flew up into the air.

THE little plane flew beautifully and the first time they passed the trap door Little Bear was able to push the lid open with his paintbrush. Then Rabbit circled the plane again, this time very close to the hole. Little Bear grabbed the edge and with a mighty heave he pulled himself inside.

He got out his torch and looked around. The attic was very dark and quiet; full of boxes, old clothes and dust. He couldn't see Old Bear at all.

'Any bears in here?' he whispered, and stood still to listen.

From somewhere quite near he heard a muffled 'Grrrrr,' followed by, 'Did somebody say something?' Little Bear moved a few things aside and there, propped up against a cardboard box and covered in dust, was Old Bear.

LITTLE Bear jumped up and down with excitement. 'Old Bear! Old Bear! I've found Old Bear!' he shouted.

'So you have,' said Old Bear.

'Have you been lonely?' asked Little Bear.

'Quite lonely,' said Old Bear. 'But I've been asleep a lot of the time.'

'Well,' said Little Bear kindly, 'would you like to come back to the playroom with us now?'

'That would be lovely,' replied Old Bear. 'But how will we get down?'

'Don't worry about that,' said Little Bear, 'Bramwell has thought of everything. He's given us these handkerchiefs to use as parachutes.'

GOOD old Bramwell,' said the old teddy. 'I'm
glad he didn't forget me.' Old Bear stood up
and shook the dust out of his fur and Little Bear
helped him into his parachute. They went over to
the hole in the ceiling.

   'Ready,' shouted Rabbit.
   'Steady,' shouted Duck.
   'GO!' shouted Bramwell Brown.

The two bears leapt bravely from the hole in the
ceiling. Their handkerchief parachutes opened out
and they floated gently down . . . landing safely
in the blanket.

WELCOME home, Old Bear,' said Bramwell
Brown, patting his friend on the back.
The others patted him too, just to make him feel
at home. 'It's nice to have you back,' they said.
'It's nice to *be* back,' replied Old Bear.

THAT night, when all the animals were tucked up in bed, Bramwell thought about the day's adventures and looked at the others.

Rabbit was dreaming exciting dreams about bouncing as high as an aeroplane.

Duck was dreaming that he could really fly and was rescuing bears from all sorts of high places.

Little Bear was dreaming of all the interesting things he had seen in the attic, and Old Bear was dreaming about the good times he would have now he was back with his friends.

'I *knew* it was going to be a special day,' said Bramwell Brown to himself.

JANE HISSEY

Little Bear's Trousers

THE sun shone through the window and woke Little Bear. 'What a lovely morning,' he said to himself. 'I'll do something different today.'

HE jumped down from the bed, took off his pyjamas and looked for his trousers.

He looked on the chair where he'd left them and he looked on the floor under the chair – and then he looked through the chest of drawers in case they were there. But they weren't. They were nowhere.

'But they must be somewhere,' said Little Bear. 'Trousers don't disappear. I'll go and ask Old Bear. *He'll* know where they are.'

OLD Bear was already enjoying the sun in his deckchair. 'I haven't seen your trousers, I'm afraid,' he said. 'But Camel was around here earlier. Perhaps she knows where they are.'

OH dear,' said Camel, when Little Bear found her a few minutes later. 'I did find them. I thought they were a pair of hump warmers and I tried them on to see if they fitted me. They did keep my humps *quite* warm but the air came down the tops so I decided these were better.' And she showed Little Bear two very smart bobble hats – one for each hump.

'I gave the old hump warmers to Sailor to use as sails for his boat. Jump on my back and let's see if we can find him.' Little Bear scrambled up and they galloped off in the direction of the bathroom.

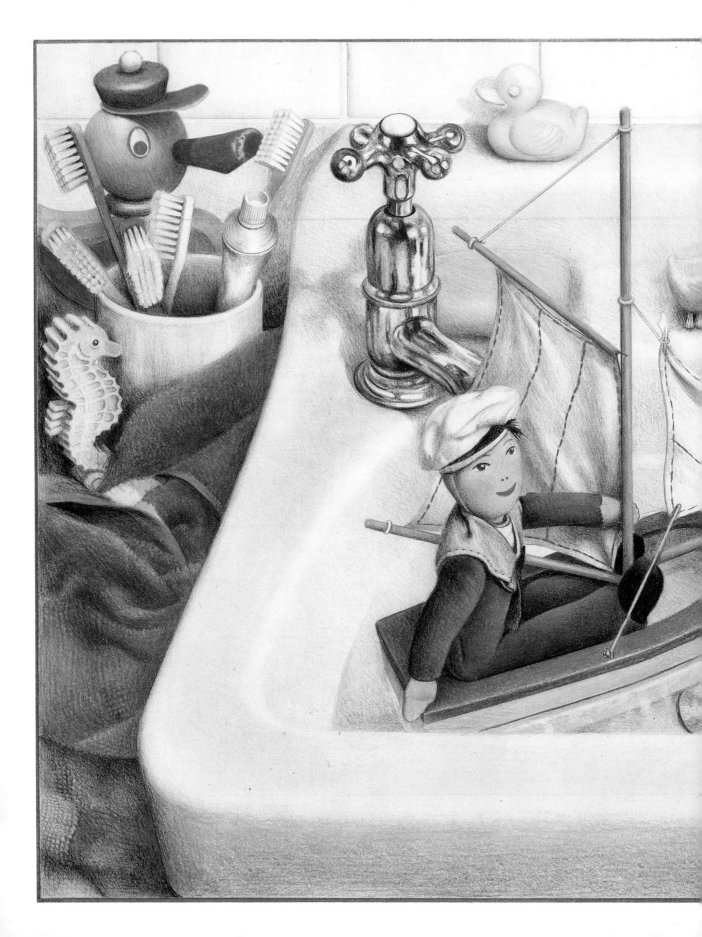

SAILOR was looking after the boats and ducks in the bathroom. 'I did use them as sails,' he said, 'but they looked too much like trousers.'

'That's because they *are* trousers,' said Little Bear crossly. 'Where are they now?'

'I gave them to Dog to keep his bones in,' said Sailor. 'Sorry, Little Bear. We'd better hurry, he might be anywhere by now.'

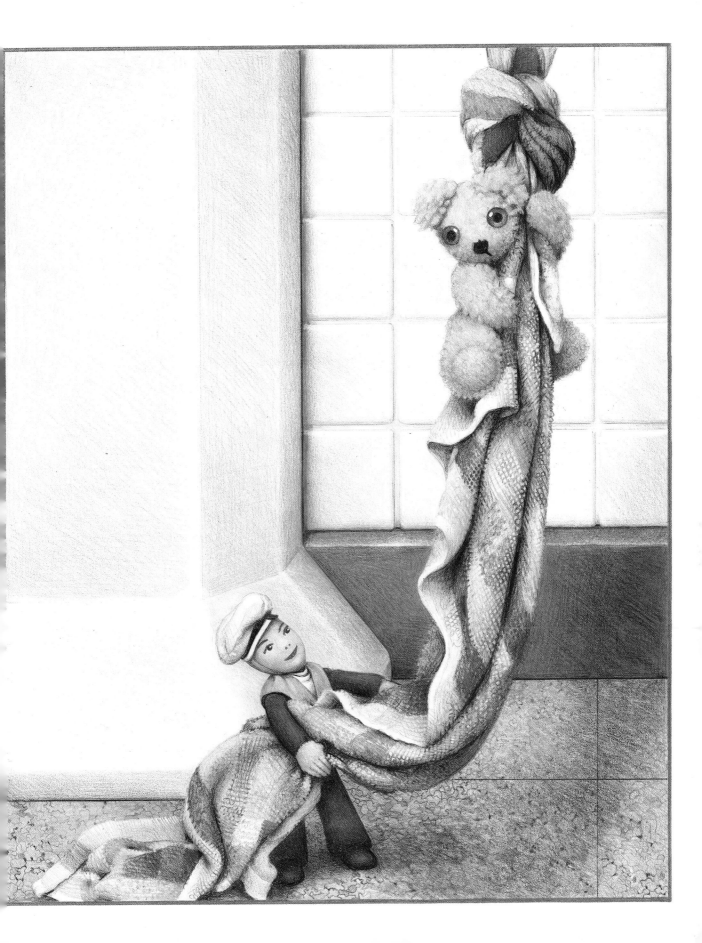

DOG was happily burying his bones in flowerpots when Little Bear found him. 'My bones kept falling through the two-bone bone-holder,' he said.

'TWO-BONE BONE-HOLDER!' cried Little Bear in dismay. 'Oh, Dog, can't you recognize trousers when you see them?'

'Oh, dear,' said Dog. 'I do feel silly. I gave them to Rabbit – he said he needed a skiing hat, and your trousers looked just perfect. I am sorry.'

WHEEE!' cried Rabbit, as he shot past Little Bear a few minutes later, skiing down the bannister on two lolly stick skis. He didn't have Little Bear's trousers on his head now.

'But I did have them earlier,' he explained when Little Bear caught up with him. 'They made a lovely rabbit hat, with plenty of room for my ears. But they slipped over my eyes and I crashed, so I decided it was safer without them. I gave them to Zebra to carry her building bricks in.'

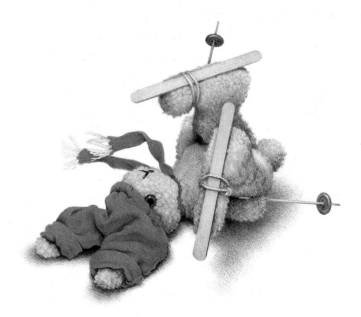

ZEBRA was building herself a house when Little Bear arrived. But his trousers were nowhere to be seen.

'I wondered whose they were,' she said. 'They were terribly useful. I tied up the legs with string, put them on my back and carried all these bricks here in them. But when I had enough bricks for my house I gave them to Duck to use as a flag for his sand castle. I am sorry, Little Bear. I didn't know they belonged to you.'

DUCK was in the sand tray looking sadly at the castle he'd made. There was no trouser flag on the top now. 'I did use the flag that Zebra gave me,' he sighed. 'But Bramwell Brown came and said it was just what he needed, urgently, in the kitchen. He gave me this paper flag to use instead.'

'Never mind,' said Little Bear with a sigh, feeling quite glad that his trousers were not covered in sand.

The kitchen was in a terrible muddle. There were bowls and spoons and eggs and flour, and in the middle of it all sat Bramwell Brown.

HE had Little Bear's trousers but, oh dear, he'd filled them with pink icing and was busy decorating a huge cake with them.

'It's a special occasion cake,' said Bramwell. 'And you have to put icing on special occasion cakes. I thought I could do two stripes at once with these icing bags.'

'But they're *not* icing bags. They are my trousers!' sniffed Little Bear, trying hard not to cry.

'I thought I'd seen them before,' said Bramwell Brown.

D ON'T worry, Little Bear,' said Old Bear, who always arrived at the right moment. 'The icing will wash out and they'll look as good as new.'

'What's the special occasion cake for?' asked Little Bear, feeling a bit more cheerful at this news.

'Well, I didn't really know,' said Bramwell. 'I just felt like making one.'

Old Bear thought hard, 'Perhaps it ought to be a Trousers Day Cake,' he suggested helpfully.

So that's what Bramwell Brown wrote on the cake. Twice. Once with the icing from the left trouser leg and once with the icing from the right trouser leg. It said, Happy Trousers Day, in the middle, and there was a trousers pattern all round the edge.

DUCK washed Little Bear's trousers and dried them next to the cooker. Then all the toys sat down to enjoy a piece of cake and to celebrate the day Little Bear lost, and found, his trousers.

AND ever since Trousers Day, Little Bear has slept with his trousers under his pillow. 'Nobody will find them there,' he says.

JANE HISSEY
Little Bear Lost

OLD Bear had been busy all morning. He'd packed an enormous picnic for all the toys. There were sandwiches, cakes, buns, pies and jellies.

'I think I've put in a bit too much food,' he said to himself as he sat on the picnic-basket lid to try to make it close.

Suddenly in a blur of fur and red trousers, Little Bear dashed past the basket and dived into a heap of books. 'Do you think anyone will find me?' he asked from the middle of the heap.

'I shouldn't think so,' said Old Bear. 'Who's looking for you?'

Bᴜᴛ before Little Bear could answer, the door flew open and into the room ran Bramwell Brown, Duck and Rabbit. They didn't seem to be looking for Little Bear and, in a moment, they were hiding too. Rabbit and Duck were behind the curtains and Bramwell's feet could just be seen sticking out from under a cushion.

'We're playing hide and seek,' explained the cushion in a Bramwell Brown sort of voice. 'Did anyone see us hide?'

'Only me,' said Old Bear, 'but who's looking for you?'

THERE was a bit of a silence and then the cushion moved.

Bramwell looked sadly up at Old Bear. 'Oh dear,' he said, miserably, 'we've done it again. We've forgotten to have a seeker in our game of hide-and-seek.'

The others crept out of their hiding places and sat down on Bramwell's cushion.

'What a pity,' said Duck. 'It could have been a good game, too.'

'Old Bear,' said Little Bear, thoughtfully, 'if we all hide again, could you look for us?'

OLD Bear said that was a good idea and, with paws over his eyes, he slowly counted to ten.

'One, two, three,' he began, as Rabbit jumped into a vase and tried to look like a bunch of flowers.

'Four, five, six,' he continued, as Duck jumped into a shoe box.

'Seven, eight, nine,' he said, giving Bramwell time to hide a last bit of paw.

'TEN,' he called; 'I'm READY!' And by then Little Bear had also disappeared.

OLD Bear looked all around the room to see whether any paws or ears were showing. It wasn't very tidy.

First he found a sock that he'd lost weeks ago. And then he found at least ten marbles that had rolled underneath things. He even found Cat, who wasn't really lost or hiding, and Cat helped him look for the others. But he couldn't find them.

'It's no good,' he sighed. 'I can't find any of you. I can only find things I'm *not* looking for. Can we tidy up a bit and then start again?'

ONE by one the other toys wriggled out of their secret hiding places. All of them, that is, except Little Bear.

'Where's Little Bear?' asked Bramwell Brown, but nobody seemed to know.

'Well he can't be far away,' said Old Bear. 'Let's give him a shout.'

They all climbed up on a chair and called 'LITTLE BEAR' so loudly that they made themselves jump and almost fell off. Duck prodded all the cushions with his beak to see whether Little Bear was underneath, and Bramwell peered under the bed.

H<small>E</small> could be under here,' he said.

'Well, I'm not going to look,' said Duck. 'It's dark and dusty.'

'Oh, I'll go,' said Rabbit. 'It's just like a tunnel and I love tunnels.' He was just about to dive under the bed when Bramwell grabbed him by the tail.

'Wait a minute, Rabbit,' he said. 'I'll give you the end of this string and then you won't get lost because we'll all be on the other end.'

With the string tied round his middle, Rabbit bounded into the darkness. The others waited and watched.

Suddenly the string gave such a jerk that Duck fell on his beak.

'He's here, he's here!' squeaked Rabbit. 'I'm holding on to him, can you pull us out?'

All together they pulled hard on the string and out popped Rabbit, tail first, clutching not Little Bear but . . .

. . . a fluffy slipper!

'Oh,' said Duck, looking down at the slipper, 'I don't think that's Little Bear.'

'Of course it's not,' said Bramwell. 'He never looked like that.'

'It *felt* like Little Bear,' said Rabbit.

'It's not your fault, Rabbit,' said Old Bear, kindly. 'You were very brave to go in there on your own and I'm sure Little Bear will turn up soon.'

'I bet he won't,' said Duck, still gazing at the slipper. 'He's probably wandered off and is miles away by now.'

'Rubbish!' said Bramwell. 'I expect he's just stuck in something. We must keep looking.'

I think we should make a poster saying "This bear is lost", with a picture of Little Bear on it,' said Old Bear. 'Then all the toys will know who we're looking for.'

The animals all fetched the painting things and Bramwell sat and painted a picture of a small bear in red trousers that did look quite a bit like Little Bear. There wasn't really enough room to write 'This bear is lost', so they just made him look a bit sad and hoped that everyone would know what it meant.

JUST to make sure, Bramwell called all the other toys together and explained what had happened. They all wanted to help and, within minutes, everyone was searching.

They rolled up rugs and climbed up curtains. They jumped into drawers and turned out toys. They peered behind plants and rummaged through rubbish.

They felt as though they'd searched through the whole house but still there was no sign of Little Bear.

PHEW, I'm tired,' said Bramwell Brown.
'And I'm hungry,' said Duck.
'Well,' said Old Bear, 'everyone has worked very hard and I think we all deserve our picnic. When we've eaten we'll start looking again.'

He led the way to the picnic basket that he'd packed in the morning and lifted the lid.

'There,' he said proudly. 'What do you think of that?'

THE animals all peered inside. But what they saw was not what they had expected to see.

There, lying tucked up under a tea cloth, fast asleep and looking very full, was Little Bear.

'Well, well!' gasped Bramwell Brown.

'Hmm, we seem to have found a bear and lost a picnic,' said Duck, staring at the crumbs that covered Little Bear.

'It's a good thing I made too much then,' said Old Bear. 'There's still plenty left for us.'

Bramwell Brown lifted Little Bear out of the basket and gave him a big hug.

'Come on everyone,' he called, 'picnic time!'

CAREFULLY, they dragged the basket bumpety bump down the stairs and out into the garden.

'This looks like a good place for a picnic,' said Old Bear, spreading the cloth out under a tree.

They had a wonderful feast, finishing every crumb in the basket. Then they stretched out in the sun to rest.

'I know,' said Little Bear, suddenly leaping to his feet, 'let's have *another* game of hide-and-seek.'

But there was no reply. Leaning against the tree and full of food, all the other toys were fast asleep.

Jane Hissey
JOLLY TALL

Bramwell Brown had been busy knitting all week. He'd started on Monday, knitted all Tuesday, and by Wednesday the scarf he was making was just about long enough for Little Bear. But Bramwell didn't stop. By Thursday the scarf fitted Rabbit and Little Bear *together*, but still Bramwell kept knitting. On Friday the scarf fitted Rabbit, Little Bear *and* Duck. But Bramwell didn't stop knitting until Saturday, and by then the scarf was too long for anyone in the playroom.

'I suppose we could cut it up,' said Little Bear. 'Then everyone would have a scarf.'

'It would all come unknitted then,' said Old Bear.

Little Bear tried on the scarf once more, but he tripped over the end and landed upside down in Bramwell's lap. 'Why did you make it so long?' he asked.

'Because people kept interrupting me,' said Bramwell, 'and I forgot to measure it.'

'Never mind,' said Old Bear. 'I'm sure it will come in useful sometime.'

'As a skipping-rope perhaps,' grumbled Duck.

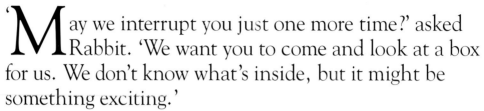

'May we interrupt you just one more time?' asked Rabbit. 'We want you to come and look at a box for us. We don't know what's inside, but it might be something exciting.'

'Like treasure,' said Little Bear.

'Probably empty,' muttered Duck. Rabbit led the toys to a tall box tied up with string. Bramwell walked all round it.

'It hasn't got a label,' he said. 'I'll make a hole in it and look inside.' With his knitting needle Bramwell poked a tiny hole in the box.

The box said 'Ouch!'

'Can boxes talk?' whispered Rabbit.

'Well this one just did,' said Little Bear.

'It wasn't the box,' said Old Bear. 'It was the something inside.'

'What a pity,' said Little Bear. 'It can't be treasure then.'

'Well it might be something *guarding* the treasure,' said Rabbit hopefully. 'Go on Bramwell, open it — please.'

Bramwell studied the mysterious package. 'I think I ought to talk to it first and see if it's friendly.' He crept over to the little hole. 'Hello,' he called softly. 'Are you friend or foe?'

'Hello,' came the muffled reply. 'I think I must be a friend because I haven't heard of a foe, unless a foe is better than a friend in which case I'm one of those.'

'It doesn't sound very sure,' said Duck.

'I think we ought to be prepared anyway,' said Rabbit. 'I'll find a net to catch it in, in case it suddenly jumps out.'

Duck fetched a rope to tie it up. 'It might escape from your net,' he said. Little Bear found a bag to put the treasure in, just in case there was some.

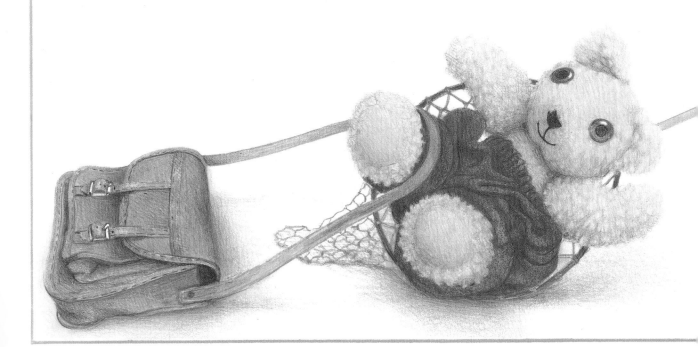

Very carefully, Bramwell and Old Bear untied the string and lifted the lid.
They all held their breath . . .
Two little furry horns appeared first, then two large furry ears, and then a great big friendly furry face.
'Oh that's better,' said the something, smiling down at the toys. 'Hello everyone, what have you got there?'

Rabbit and Duck quickly dropped the net and the rope, but Little Bear clung hopefully to his bag.

'Excuse me,' he said, 'are you standing on some treasure?'

The big furry head disappeared into the box and then popped out again. 'Sorry,' it said, 'there's no treasure in here.'

'What are you standing on then?' asked Rabbit.

'Just the bottom of the box,' it replied.

'Gosh!' gasped Little Bear. 'You must be jolly tall.'

'That's right,' said their new friend. 'I'm Jolly Tall, that's my name, but you can call me Jolly if you like. Do you like my house?'

'Well actually,' said Little Bear, 'we thought it was just a box. It would look better with doors and windows.'

Jolly agreed, so the toys set to work. Little Bear cut out the windows and doors, Bramwell fetched some material for the curtains, and Rabbit fixed them in place with glue and pins. All the toys helped, and were very pleased when at last the box looked like a real house. Little Bear went in to tell Jolly that it was ready. 'You can come out now,' he said.

'I'm afraid I can't,' said Jolly. 'I'm too tall for the front door.'

'You could *jump* out,' suggested Rabbit.

Jolly jumped, but he couldn't get anywhere near high enough. Little Bear rushed out of the door very quickly; a jumping Jolly seemed more dangerous than a still one.

'Fetch the crane!' said Old Bear. 'We'll *lift* you out.'

'Will that mean going up?' asked Jolly nervously.

'Of course,' said Old Bear. 'Up and over the top of the box.'

'But I don't like heights,' said Jolly. 'My head seems to think it's high enough as it is.'

'I know what to do,' said Little Bear, 'I'll put my paws over your eyes. Then you won't see how high you're going.'
Puffing and panting, the toys managed to lift the cranc up on to a pile of books to make it taller than Jolly Tall. Little Bear tied the chain to a handkerchief around Jolly's middle, climbed up Jolly's neck, and leaned over to cover his eyes with his paws.

'We're ready,' he shouted, and Bramwell began to turn the handle of the crane.

Very slowly, Jolly began to rise out of the box, and soon the toys could see nearly all of his long neck. Feeling very excited, Bramwell wound the handle around faster and faster as more and more of Jolly appeared.

'We're up,' cried Little Bear, taking one paw off Jolly's eye to wave to the others.

Then it happened . . . .

J olly saw how high up he was and began to wave his legs
about like a windmill — the box wobbled, Jolly
wobbled, and both went crashing to the floor. Little Bear
flew across the room and disappeared. But nobody
noticed; they were too busy pulling Jolly out of his box.

The toys helped Jolly up and on to his feet again.

'But where's Little Bear?' they asked, anxiously peering into the battered box.

'I'm here,' came a little voice from across the room. 'I
flew.' There was Little Bear, clinging to the playroom
curtain by the tips of his paws. 'Help!' he shouted. 'I
can't get down.'

'Hang on,' said Jolly, galloping to the rescue. 'I think I
can get you down. You can slide down my neck.'

Little Bear could hang on no longer. He let go of the curtain, shot all the way down Jolly's neck and fell, plop, into the net that Bramwell held out for him. He enjoyed it so much that he wanted another go, but Old Bear said it was time for bed.

'W here's Jolly going to sleep?' asked Rabbit.
'I'll swap my bed for your house, Jolly,' said Little
Bear.

'You can *have* my house,' said Jolly cheerfully. 'Giraffes
sleep standing up; just a blanket would
do for me.'

Rabbit and Little Bear found a nice
cosy blanket for their new friend. But they
couldn't get all of him under it. 'Your neck's
going to get cold,' sighed Little Bear.

Bramwell looked at Jolly with
his neck sticking out of
the blanket.

'Just a moment,' he cried
rushing off. A few minutes
later he returned with a carefully
wrapped parcel.

'It's a present for you, Jolly,'
he said. 'A *welcome* present.'

Jolly unwrapped the parcel. Inside was the very, very long red scarf. 'It's lovely,' he said. 'It's the best welcome present ever. But how did you know I'd need it?'

'We knew *someone* would,' said Bramwell, and he wound the extra long scarf round and round and round Jolly's long neck.

'We thought you were a box of treasure this morning,' said Rabbit.

'Or just an empty box,' said Duck.

'But we're very glad you weren't,' said Little Bear. 'A new friend is much more fun than a whole boxful of treasure!'

Jane Hissey
JOLLY SNOW

It was cold and grey outside. Jolly Tall, the giraffe, had been gazing out of the window for days.

'What are you waiting for?' asked Rabbit.

'I'm waiting for it to snow,' said Jolly. 'It is winter isn't it?'

'It doesn't *always* snow in winter,' said Rabbit.

'In fact it hardly ever does,' said Duck gloomily.

'I know where there's some snow,' said Little Bear. 'It must be left over from last winter. I'll get it for you.'

Without waiting to explain, Little Bear rushed out of the room.

In a moment he was back again carrying a large glass bubble. Inside the bubble they could see a little house and a tree covered in a layer of tiny white snowflakes.

'Is that all snow does?' asked Jolly staring into the bubble. 'Does it just lie around making things whiter than usual?'

'Of course not,' said Little Bear. 'That wouldn't be any fun. You can make it into balls and throw it.'

'Or slide on it,' said Zebra.

'And jump into heaps of it,' said Rabbit, 'and make footprints.'

'You can build things with it too,' said Duck.

'Goodness,' said Jolly. 'There doesn't look enough of it for that.'

Holding the glass bubble tightly, Little Bear jumped up and down. A flurry of snowflakes leaped from the tiny house and tree and rushed around inside the glass. 'Look at it now!' he squeaked.

   'There's still not enough to make a snowball,' said Jolly.

   'And anyway you can't get it out,' said Duck.

   'Wait a minute,' said Zebra, 'I know where there's lots of snow.'

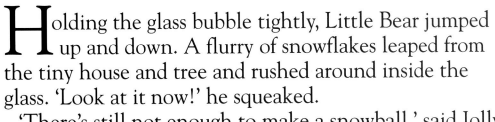

She led the way to the kitchen, where Bramwell
Brown was busy making some special biscuits. To
stop the biscuit dough sticking to the rolling pin, he was
shaking flour from a flour shaker.

'Whoopee!' cried Zebra, dashing under the falling flour.
'I'm in a snowstorm.'

In no time at all, her black stripes had almost
disappeared.

Rabbit tried to gather up a pawful of the flour. 'It's not very good for snowballs,' he said. 'It doesn't stick together.'

'But it's perfect for DOUGHBALLS,' cried Little Bear, rolling up a piece of dough and throwing it at Rabbit. The doughball stuck to Rabbit's bottom and looked like an extra tail.

'This flour-snow doesn't come off,' said Zebra, jumping up and down trying to shake herself clean.

'I think you are going to need a bath,' said Bramwell.

He filled a dish with soapy water and the snowy Zebra climbed in. She began to splash about sending bubbles flying everywhere. 'It's still not coming off,' she grumbled. 'It just gets stickier and stickier.'

'Flour and water make a sort of glue,' said Duck. 'You'll probably have to stay white for ever.'

'No you won't,' said Bramwell kindly. 'We'll get you clean.'

All the scrubbing and splashing made even more bubbles.

'Snow-bubbles!' cried Little Bear, jumping about, popping them with his paws. 'Hurry up Zebra, we want to use your bath as a snow-machine.'

After lots of rubbing and scrubbing, Zebra's stripes at last reappeared. The others wrapped her in a warm towel and looked into the bath.

'What have you done with all the bubbles?' asked Little Bear.

'Bubbles never last,' said Duck, 'and anyway they would have made very sloppy snow. Why don't we go and see if Old Bear has any ideas?'

Old Bear was in the dining room cutting out paper decorations. He'd made paper stars, paper bells and paper lanterns. He'd even made paper snowflakes.

'You can't really play with these,' said Little Bear, trying to slide on a snowflake.

'No you can't,' said Old Bear rescuing his decoration. 'They're only meant for looking at.'

'We want some snow for Jolly,' said Rabbit. 'Snow you *can* play with.'

'What about these?' said Old Bear scattering a blizzard of paper pieces in the air.

'Lovely,' said Rabbit.

'And nice and slippery too,' said Little Bear, taking a run at a heap of them and skidding along on his bottom.

'What we need is a sledge,' said Rabbit, 'or Little Bear will wear out his trousers.' He fetched a cardboard box and Bramwell cut away the sides. Duck tied a string to the front and they pulled it along to test it.

'Now if we had a slope,' said Rabbit, 'we could whizz down it in the sledge.'

'I don't think I could,' said Jolly. 'I wouldn't fit in it.'

'Never mind,' said Bramwell. 'You can help with the slope.' Bramwell Brown disappeared into the bedroom and came back pulling a large white sheet. He gave a corner to Jolly. 'Now,' said Bramwell, 'when the others climb on, lift up your end and they should slide all the way down.'

Rabbit and Little Bear pushed the sledge onto the sheet and climbed in.

'There's only room for two,' said Rabbit.

'Don't worry,' said Zebra, 'I'll slide on my tummy.'

As soon as they were ready, Little Bear called out to Jolly: 'One, two, three, GO!'

Jolly and Bramwell lifted their end of the sheet. Nothing happened.

'Wobble it a bit,' called Rabbit. 'We seem to be stuck.' Jolly and Bramwell shook the sheet as hard as they could and suddenly the toys found themselves sliding very fast to the other end.

'Look out,' cried Little Bear as the sledge whizzed off the sheet, across the room and crashed into the wall on the other side.

'I think we need a softer landing,' said Rabbit, fluffing up his flattened fur and helping Little Bear to his feet. He piled up a heap of cushions against the wall and then all three toys bravely climbed back onto the sheet.

'Ready, steady, go!' they called to Jolly.

Up went the sheet. Down went the toys – straight into the heap of cushions. As they landed clouds of feathers puffed out of a little hole in one of the cushions and filled the room.

'Look – it's feather-snow,' cried Little Bear, making the hole bigger with his paw and jumping on the cushion to make more feathers escape. Very soon all the toys were jumping in the feathers. They rolled in them, crawled through them and piled them in heaps.

'Is this like snow?' asked Jolly.

'It's better,' said Little Bear. 'It doesn't melt and it doesn't make you cold.'

'Let's put some round the windows,' suggested Rabbit, 'then it will look as if real snow has settled there.'

He climbed up to the windowsill and began to pile feathers in each corner. When he reached the third window pane he stopped and looked, then looked again.

'Somebody has already done this one,' he called to the others. The window did have a white covering around the edges . . . but it was on the *outside*.

'It isn't feathers,' cried Little Bear excitedly, 'it's real snow!'

All the toys crowded onto the sill and stared out of the window in amazement.

'Now we can play outside,' said Zebra.

'Well, actually – it looks a bit deep for me,' said Little Bear.

'And a bit cold for me,' said Old Bear.

At that moment, Bramwell Brown came into the room carrying a huge plateful of his special snowflake biscuits.

'I think what you need is some of *my* snow,' he said.

Jolly Tall thought about the flour-snow and the feather-snow, the bubble-snow and the paper-snow. Then he looked at the real snow floating down outside.

'I really like all kinds of snow,' he announced. 'But,' he added, munching a snowflake biscuit, 'Bramwell's snow is probably the snow I like best!'